PELICAN AND PELICANT

Written by Sarah Froeber

Illustrated by Kim Mosher

Toucan Press, Inc.
Chapel Hill, North Carolina

Published by
Toucan Press, Inc.
P.O. Box 16112
Chapel Hill, NC 27516
toucanpress@aol.com
www.pelicanandpelicant.com

Library of Congress Card Number: 2003111980

ISBN 0-9744926-0-4

Second Edition

Printed in the United States of America

This book is dedicated to
Jef, Scraps the cat,
and all of the beautiful pelicans in our lives
who inspire, encourage and assist us.

On the island of Buxtonia, there once lived two very different birds. The first bird was eager and self-confident and so was called Pelican. If she had the chance to do something new, or meet someone new, or visit a new place, she would take a deep breath and stretch out her wings and shout, "I CAN!"

The other bird was nervous about doing new things, or meeting new animals, or going to new places. She was called Pelicant. In any strange situation, she would hold her breath and hide her head under her wing and whisper, "I can't."

When Pelican discovered a gigantic oak tree in the middle of the island, she said to herself, "I have never perched at the top of such a big tree before." The idea of sitting up in the air filled her with delight. She took a deep breath and stretched out her wings and shouted, "I CAN!" Then she flew to the highest branch of the enormous oak.

The branch felt strong and
sturdy under her feet, and its leaves
tickled her feathers. "Super grouper!"
she exclaimed. "I can see the whole island
from up here, and I can rest at the same time!"
Pelican looked all around. "There is the
lighthouse, and there is Turtle's pond, and there is
Pelicant's nest." Pelican called down to Pelicant, "Come
up here! Quick! Come and look! You can see all the way to the
lighthouse from this tree."

TURTLE POND

Pelicant held
her breath and
hid her head
under her wing and
whispered, "I can't.
I might get dizzy up so
high, and I might fall off
the branch and hurt
myself, and I might get
pecked by a woodpecker!"
So while Pelican perched on the
highest branch of the enormous
oak tree and looked out over
all of Buxtonia,

Pelicant sat in her nest alone.

When Goose moved into a nest near Pelican's home, Pelican said to herself, "A new friend!" The thought of making a new friend filled Pelican with delight. She took a deep breath and stretched out her wings and shouted, "I CAN!"

Then she flew over and introduced herself. "Hi! My name is Pelican. Welcome to Buxtonia."

"Thank you so much," Goose honked, shaking wings with Pelican. "I came here from the Far North, but I was afraid I might not be welcome. In some places they do not like geese."

"Not here," Pelican insisted. "This is a friendly island. Would you like me to show you around?"

Goose clapped his wings together.
"Yes," he honked, and off they went.

"That is the lighthouse," Pelican pointed out as they flew by. "And that is the oak tree where I perch, and that is the pond where my friend Turtle lives."

Pelican took her
new friend Goose to the beach.
They wrote their names in the sand with their
wings. They glided in the air currents over the waves.
They splashed water on each other until they were both soaking
wet. Then the birds stretched out on the warm sand to dry.

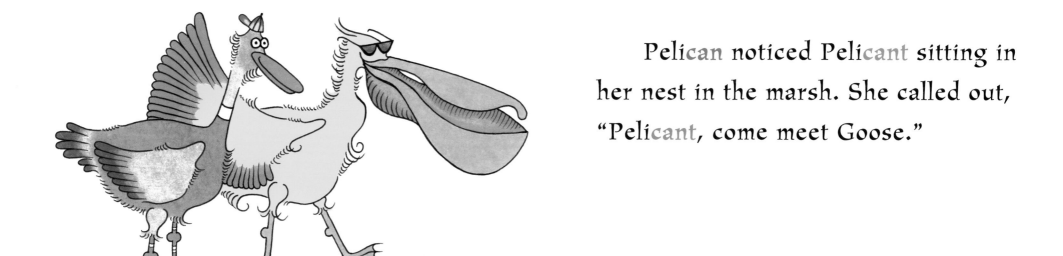

Pelican noticed Pelicant sitting in her nest in the marsh. She called out, "Pelicant, come meet Goose."

Pelicant held her breath and hid her head under her wing and whispered, "I can't. Goose might not like me, and he might play too rough, and I might not be able to understand the way he talks!"

So while Pelican played at the beach with her new friend,

Pelicant sat in her nest alone.

When Turtle told Pelican about all the fish in the ocean off Ocracokia Island, Pelican said to herself, "I have never been to Ocracokia!" The idea of going to a new place filled her with delight. She took a deep breath and stretched out her wings and shouted, "I CAN!"

Circling Pelicant's nest, Pelican called out,
"Pelicant, come with me to Ocracokia. The
fishing there is supposed to be super grouper!"

Pelicant held her breath and hid her head under her wing and whispered, "I can't. My wings might get tired from all that flying, and I might not like the way those fish taste, and I might not be able to find my way home."

Pelican flew to Ocracokia and found huge schools of fish feeding in the ocean there. Every time Pelican plunge-dived, she caught a fish. By the end of the day she had eaten so much that she had to sit on the water and rest for two hours before she could fly home.

While Pelican floated on the waves remembering her delicious meal,

Pelicant sat in her nest alone.

One beautiful summer day, Turtle planned a party to celebrate her forty-third birthday. All the animals in Buxtonia were invited.

When Pelican received her invitation, she said to herself, "Super grouper! I bet Turtle will have a crab birthday cake with crayfish frosting, and I bet we play Pin-the-Fin-on-the-Dolphin, and I bet there will be lots of singing and dancing."

The thought of going to Turtle's party filled her with delight. She took a deep breath and stretched out her wings and shouted, "I CAN!"

She washed her feathers, and shined her beak, and set off for the festivities, carrying a birthday poem she had written for Turtle under her wing.

The poem read:

"Turtle, every year you get more and more wise. Happy Birthday to you from your friend who flies!"

Pelican

On the way, Pelican passed by Pelicant's nest.
"Pelicant, are you coming to Turtle's party?" she asked.

Pelicant held her breath and hid her head under her wing and whispered, "I can't. The other animals at the party might not talk to me, and they might not like the way my beak looks, and they might think my feathers are not clean enough, and I don't know how to dance, and I don't have a present to give Turtle."

So Pelican flew as fast as she could to Turtle's pond,

and Pelicant sat in her nest alone.

Pelican arrived at the party and sang out, "Happy birthday, Turtle!"

Turtle smiled. "Thank you for coming to my party. Is Pelicant coming?"

Pelican shook her head. "No. I do not understand that bird. She never wants to do anything. She just sits in her nest by herself."

"Maybe she needs a friend to help her," suggested Turtle. "She might not be so nervous about doing new things, or going to new places, or meeting new animals if she had someone with her."

"Yes!" Pelican agreed. "Someone to help her feel safe!"

"Pelicant would feel safe with you," Turtle said.

"Maybe I could bring her to the party," Pelican said to herself. The idea of being with her friend filled Pelican with delight. She took a deep breath and stretched out her wings and shouted, "I CAN!"

She hurried back to Pelicant's nest. "I would like you to come to the birthday party with me," Pelican said. "You do not have to worry about having someone to talk to because I will talk to you. I like talking to you. You know a lot of really interesting things. In fact, you are an expert on nests!"

Pelicant giggled.

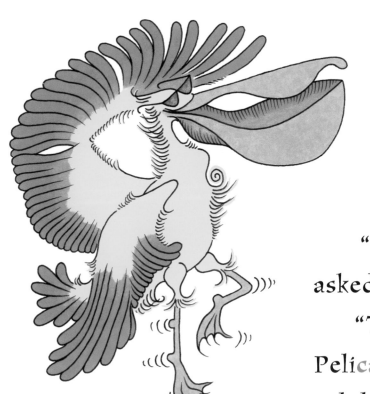

"I know a lot of dances, too," said Pelican. "I can teach you the Pelican Pop-up. It is very fun. You crouch down and then you pop up on one leg. You would be super grouper at it because you have such good balance."

"But what about a birthday present for Turtle?" Pelicant asked. "I don't have anything to give her."

"The best present you could give Turtle," Pelican assured Pelicant, "is to go to her party. She wants to have friends with her to celebrate her birthday. Turtle wants that more than anything."

Pelicant stood up, almost convinced. Then she touched her beak self-consciously, looked at her feathers, and plopped down in her nest again.

"Your beak looks very shiny to me," Pelican said. "And your feathers are clean and fluffy. But Pelicant, it is not how you look on the outside that matters. It is how much you love that counts. I believe you have a very loving heart."

"Thank you." Pelicant's eyes glistened with tears. She was quiet for a moment, and then she decided, "Okay. I'll go. But I'm still a little nervous. Will you stay close by me at the party?"

Pelican wrapped her wing around Pelicant. "Yes, I will," she said.

The two birds walked wing-in-wing to Turtle's pond.

Arriving at the party, Pelican sang out, "Happy birthday again, Turtle! Look who I brought with me."

Turtle smiled and said, "I am so glad you came to my party, Pelicant. You have made me very happy."

Pelicant ducked her head under her wing and whispered, "Happy birthday, Turtle." She felt very shy at first, but with Pelican close by, she soon felt safe enough to join in the festivities.

Pelicant talked to the other guests at the party, and ate crab birthday cake with crayfish frosting, and came in second place in the Pin-the-Fin-on-the-Dolphin game. She even danced the Pelican Pop-up, and everyone who watched complimented her on her excellent balance.

When the party ended, Pelicant told Pelican, "Thank you for helping me." She took a deep breath and stretched out her wings and shouted, "I HAD SO MUCH FUN!"

Now on the island of Buxtonia, there live two birds who like doing new things, and meeting new animals, and going to new places. Sometimes they want to have a friend along, and sometimes they feel safe enough to try new things on their own. But whether they are alone or together, these two birds are known throughout the island as the super grouper Pelicans.